The Witch's Vacation

Story and pictures by NORMAN BRIDWELL

SCHOLASTIC INC.

New York Toronto London Auckland Sydney

For Joseph

ISBN 0-590-40558-6

12 11 10 9 8 7 6 5 4 3 2 1   7 8 9/8 0 1 2/9

Printed in the U.S.A.   24
First Scholastic printing, June 1987

We know a witch! She lives next door.
My brother and I have so much fun with
her, we never like to go away from home.

But last summer we had to go to camp. We felt bad because the witch wasn't coming with us.

It was raining when we got to camp. They gave us a tent number. But when we saw the tent, we were afraid to go inside.

What a surprise!

We put on our bathing suits and went up on the porch with the other campers. We wished it would stop raining. Then I saw something funny. In one spot on the beach it was not raining at all. And guess who was there waving at us?

We were so glad that our witch was with us again.
The other kids thought she was funny-looking.
One of them made fun of her bathing suit.

The witch just smiled and turned him into a terrific swimmer.

But just for a minute. Then she gave all the
kids some water wings to play with.

My brother built a sand castle, but a big
kid knocked it down. It didn't matter. . . .

The witch helped my brother build another sand castle.

The next day she packed a picnic basket. We ate on her picnic tablecloth.

Then everyone hiked to Lookout Point. The big kids left us far behind. The witch just smiled. She said WE would get to the top first.

UP
→
HOLD
RAIL

One night the cook couldn't get the campfire going. It looked as if we would not have a weenie roast that night.

Our good old witch came to the rescue.

Having a witch at camp makes a big difference.
It was turning out to be a wonderful vacation.

Our witch was there the day I wanted to go riding. There was just one horse left. The kids called her "Old Nellie-Bones."

I called her "Nellie the Great."

And she was.

One day I took out a rowboat so my brother could go fishing. He wasn't having much luck until . . .

the witch let him use her broom
for a fishing pole.

After a while, the witch went ashore
to take a nap.

We were having so much fun that we didn't
see where we were going.

There was a waterfall ahead and we couldn't stop.

We tried the witch's broom. It only works
for witches.

I wished for the witch as hard as I could.

Back at the camp the witch woke up. She
knew we were in trouble.

But she didn't have her broom. How could
she get to us in time?

In a wink, she changed the water to ice—

and rushed to save us. Good old witch.